# No Time To Say Goodbye

# Bill Adler Jr.

Claren Books
www.clarenbooks.com

Cover design by Fiona Jayde
Fiona Jayde Media
fionajaydemedia.com

ISBN-10: 1-945259-05-1
ISBN-13: 978-1-945259-05-0

# CONTENTS

# CHAPTER 1
## TODAY

*I*'m *too young to get up in the middle of the night to pee,* forty-year-old Dennis Tanner told himself as his feet recoiled from the cold, wooden floor at 3:03 a.m. He glanced at his wife, wrapped in a tender dream, head cradled on her pillow, and envied her sleep before obeying his bladder's merciless command to visit the bathroom.

The clock's LED light provided more than ample illumination for Dennis to navigate from bed to bathroom, even for his comatose eyes. Blue light danced around his shadow, a ghostly glow that followed his footsteps. He remembered the two beers he had drunk before bedtime and was relieved to know that it was foolishness and not a premature change in biology that had wakened him. *I've got a decade left before I start making regular middle-of-the-night treks across a cold floor,* he thought. Although he was thirsty, he decided that under the circumstances, drinking a glass of water after the bathroom visit would not be a wise idea.

Dennis headed back to bed via the two area rugs, taking a giant step from one to the other. He padded through the bedroom softly so as not to wake Rachel, who slept as a bear does in the heart of winter—motionless, suspended in perpetual night.

*5:57 a.m.? What? How can that be?* Dennis shouted in his head when he saw the night table clock. He opened

1

his eyes wide as if that would allow him to see new and better information. But the numbers didn't change, even after several hard and deliberate blinks. Somehow, almost three hours had passed since he'd gotten up.

Like a fallen mountain climber holding onto his emergency rope, whenever he woke at an ungodly hour, Dennis did everything he could to cling to somnolence. He was not one of those people who checked Facebook or email when something natural, like his bladder, or unnatural, like the upstairs neighbor rearranging his furniture in the middle of the night, disturbed his sleep. Dennis had friends who narrated their dreams in 140 characters and clicked thumbs up on Facebook during the time of day best suited for bats. But not him. Sleep was his Xanadu, magic elixir, tropical paradise. Dennis collected sleep hours like some people collect stamps or cats: the more, the better. Maybe he relished sleep because of an immutable genetic makeup or maybe it was because he resented—no, make that hated—the insane sleep deprivation he'd suffered during his five years of hospital residency. *No, doctors do not need to learn to function on almost no sleep. Nobody would ever propose similar stupidity for airline pilots, teachers, dog trainers, circus acrobats, or chefs.*

Whatever the reason, once asleep, Dennis liked to continue his hibernation for as long as the next day's schedule would permit.

*Did I fall asleep while standing at the toilet?* Dennis demanded of his subconscious. Sleeping while standing, especially for nearly three hours, was impossible, so whatever Dennis had been doing, it had only started with standing. When humans sleep, their muscles relax, which means that full-on sleep while standing is going to bring your face in close contact with the floor in a matter of minutes. Unlike horses, which can lock their knees and sleep standing up, a human's leg muscles and joints won't stay rigid while sleeping. If you don't crash to the ground—and Dennis had not—the only available activity is sleepwalking. But rarely does anyone sleepwalk longer than thirty minutes. Dennis tried to replay the previous three hours but could recall only the past five minutes from his brain's recording system.

*It's probably just a clock malfunction. Everything is fine,* Dennis concluded as he fumbled for his cellphone on the night table. But his phone confirmed 5:57 a.m. *I really did fall asleep while standing. I must be more sleep-deprived than I imagined. I've never done that before.* Dennis wasn't taking any sleep medicines, like Ambien, that made people do strange things, such as cook a meal or go for a drive—and not remember any of it. He checked his hands and feet anyway to confirm that there were no signs of nocturnal wandering. There was no dirt on his feet, no food on his hands; there were no gummy stains on his pajamas from a midnight refrigerator raid. *I was sleepwalking. Sleepwalking in circles around the bedroom and bathroom, over and over. For three hours.*

Dennis made himself promise never to drink two beers before bedtime ever again, but in his disheveled state, he could have made himself swear to give up bacon and Netflix, too.

Still wary of his main alarm clock, he set the phone's alarm for 7:00 a.m. as a backup. The small clock icon on the top bar reassured him that he'd wake—again—but this time when he needed to.

Another hour of sleep was better than no more sleep. If Dennis had had surgery scheduled, he would have already been awake. *Rise and shine, Dr. Tanner, it's a surgery day. You'll be fully awake after coffee at home and two more at the hospital.* But Dennis' Tuesday was going to be thick with office visits and consultations—no surgeries. As much as he enjoyed the operating room, the concert hall where he was both maestro and lead musician, he also savored those days when he didn't have to wake up at 5:00 a.m. for an 8:00 a.m.

operation. *That's another old-school medical practice that needs the ax. Surgery should start at a decent hour, like 10:00 a.m. Surely I'm not the only physician or nurse who would benefit from waking later.*

At 6:00 a.m., Dennis slipped back into his wife-warmed bed, pulled the down quilt over his chest, a sensation that was a prelude to being covered by sleep itself, leaned over to kiss the back of Rachel's neck, slid close so that his legs folded into hers, and instantly fell back asleep.

"You set two alarms?" Rachel asked as a cacophony of bells and buzzers filled their bedroom. She was already looking at Dennis, lying on her side, head propped up on her elbow, her voice soft and melodic. The strong morning sun played with the curtains, creating a kaleidoscopic light show that danced on the walls. Dennis blinked before he looked at the bedside clock and his phone, both of which announced 7:00 a.m.'s unwelcome arrival.

"Sorry," Dennis said as he reached for Rachel's hand. "I set my phone's alarm because I thought that the night table clock was broken. It's not, though." Dennis twisted his nose to the side as if to punctuate his apology.

"No harm, no foul," Rachel said before she leaned over to kiss him, softly and fully on the lips. Dennis returned the kiss, slid his hand under her pajamas, roamed over to her back, and pulled her close to him. "I guess setting two alarms was my soul telling me how great it is to wake up with my beautiful wife."

Rachel smiled. "For that sweet compliment, I'll make breakfast while you shower." Dennis watched as Rachel got out of bed, her long blond hair falling over her shoulders, her breasts visible through the partially unbuttoned pajama top. He wished they could both stay home in bed today. He knew that Rachel wished that, too.

"Elio's tonight?" Rachel suggested as Dennis gathered his keys and wallet for work. He checked his wallet for singles, the currency of hospital vending machines, and answered, "How about if I cook Italian, instead? I'll be home earlyish."

"Fusilli with pesto? A side of veggies made any way Dr. Chef wants."

"Your wish is my command. And garlic bread, too, will be on tonight's menu."

"The more garlicky, the better. Super-garlic."

"Now I remember why I married you," Dennis said as he pulled the door shut from the outside. Just before it closed, Dennis stuck his foot in the gap and shouted, "Wait!"

"What?" Rachel's face went pale, and her pupils dilated. "What's the matter?"

"If we're going to have all that garlic tonight, we'd better kiss once more now while we can."

⚬⚬⚬

Heart and brain surgeons get all the glory. On television, anyway. But it's general surgeons who perform every other miracle in the operating room. General surgeons are the workhorses of hospitals. If there's a problem with the esophagus, stomach, small bowel, colon, liver, pancreas, gallbladder, or thyroid gland, it's a general surgeon's job to repair that organ. Everything from hernias, which can be done under a local anesthesia and are scheduled weeks in advance, to trauma surgery—hours of grueling, bloody, life or death operations that happen without warning—falls under the general surgeon's umbrella. General surgeons are also transplant surgeons. Some doctors could forget all about anatomy, but not general surgeons, who know anatomy like London cabbies know London—no GPS allowed.

Dr. Dennis Tanner's first appointment that day was at 9:30 with Ellie Pomeroy, Ph.D., who, despite her academic skills, was no more and definitely no less nervous about having her gallbladder removed than any other breed of patient. The unconscious foot tapping, the deep breathing, like when your doctor puts a stethoscope to your chest and says "take a deep breath," the furtive eyes searching for only good news—Dennis was used to seeing these signs in his patients. Whether you're a medical doctor or a doctor of economics, as Pomeroy was, the more you think about your impending surgery, the more anxious you become. Surgery is the elephant that nobody can force out of the room until it's forced to leave.

The morning sun warmed Dennis' neck and head. He liked this time of day in autumn. It was like seeing a rainbow or finishing a meal with a silky, chocolate dessert—fleeting but wonderful. The coruscating sunlight struck his body just long enough to share with him some of its energy.

Dennis' thick, burgundy leather chair emitted a slight, high-pitched squeak as he leaned back. Dennis noticed Pomeroy glancing around his office and realized that, unlike most of his patients, she could probably understand the Latin on his various diplomas and certificates. Maybe that reassured her. Her eyes darted from diploma to window: Dennis deliberately faced his desk away from the window so his patients could look outside. Seeing the occasional hawk, swirling clouds, iconic and modern buildings, and even pigeons, calmed patients. He liked the tenth-floor view of New York and often swiveled his chair around to look outside when he was alone, but it was better that patients had that view during appointments.

Gallstones were killing forty-five-year-old Ellie Pomeroy."I feel like I'm being stoned to death from the inside, Dr. Tanner," Pomeroy said. "Big, hot…" She put her hand on her stomach, grimaced, bent over, and let out a prolonged, pained, "ouch" before continuing. "Big, burning stones being tossed around inside me. It's especially bad after a meal."

Pain was what impelled such patients to the ER with full-throated screams, only to discover that they didn't have a sudden-onset inoperable tumor.

Dennis knew that for patients like Pomeroy, tomorrow wasn't soon enough for her surgery, so he did the best he could to schedule it as quickly as possible, even if that meant less sleep for him. Dennis held up Pomeroy's X-ray to the light one last time and then asked, "How is the day after tomorrow for your gallbladder removal? You'll need to be in the hospital by 6:00 a.m., and you won't be able to eat anything after 9:00 p.m. the previous night."

"Yes," she said, unequivocally and without a moment's hesitation. Pomeroy nodded several times for emphasis. "Just tell me what to do and when to do it, and I'll be here." Pomeroy smiled, which Dennis knew was not an easy thing for somebody with gallstones to do. He relished those moments when his patients smiled because smiles and surgery rarely coexist in the same place and time.

Dennis was surprised to see his secretary walk into his office unannounced. She pushed the door open with the fury of a sudden wind gust in an equally unforeseen thunderstorm. In the six years she had worked for Dennis, the only other time she had barged into his office without intercoming first was when her husband had died. But her expression, demeanor, and even the way that she had opened the door on that sad day was the polar opposite of today. Two years before, Dennis had seen his office door creep open slowly as if there were a feeble mouse struggling to get inside. Today, there was deliberate harshness in Deidre's movements. She was hyperventilating. Dennis could almost see steam coming from her nose like a horse's in winter. Deidre stared at him, her jaw tensed and arms rigid, as if she was about to accuse him of medical malpractice or murder, and asked in a brusque, uncharacteristic tone, "Dr. Tanner? Where have you been all day?"

"Excuse me?" Dennis' head jerked up from looking at his desk.

"You missed three patient appointments and your meeting with Dr. Jansen, which had been scheduled for 4:00 p.m." She rapidly tapped her foot. "Are you all right, doctor?" Deidre moved her eyes over Dennis, like a slow-scan medical machine.

"I'm all right," Dennis said. "I feel fine." *Fine, but confused.*

He looked at his Rolex Submariner, a fifth-anniversary present from Rachel. The watch's Mercedes hands were unequivocal: 9:55 a.m. His meeting with Pomeroy had just ended. Deidre had to be the one who was confused. *Am I working her too hard and not noticing? When was her last vacation?*

Dennis looked at Deidre with sympathetic eyes, then surveyed his office. His wonderful watch said one thing, but his desk clock, displaying 5:05 p.m. in bold digits, and the sun's afternoon shadows, hatching from the west, vehemently disagreed. Dennis took his phone out of his pocket. He kept his phone off his desk during meetings with patients to avoid the phone's dark temptations, to give patients his full attention. Still certain that his phone and Rolex would agree, as they always had, he quickly pressed the phone's power button. But his phone also contradicted his watch: 5:05 p.m. The numbers burned into his retina by the phone's bright light. Just to be sure that he wasn't going insane, or maybe to confirm that he was and skip all the unpleasantness that accompanies unrelenting ambiguity, Dennis asked Deirdre, "What time is it?"

She looked at her watch, then double checked it. "It's five after five." Deidre's Australian accent almost made the time sound charming.

"Five after five," Dennis repeated to himself. He involuntarily looked at his watch again. "I don't understand."

"Doctor?"

"Did you see me at all today? After my meeting with Ellie Pomeroy, that is?" Dennis stroked his phone nervously. He hoped that the entire past minute's conversation had been some kind of wild mistake.

"I didn't see you again after your gallbladder appointment. I opened the door to your office several times, but you weren't here. I called your cell, but there was no answer."

Dennis was glad that Deidre hadn't called Rachel. He didn't want Rachel to worry or become upset about something that was a mystery to him. He preferred to present the problem and its solution at the same time. Worry should be something that's in the past, not the present.

At that moment, Dennis' phone beeped, sang, and vibrated. The unexpected dissonance made him drop the phone onto his desk. He looked at the notification bar: Thirteen voice mail messages. Twenty-seven texts. Countless emails. All arrived now. *How? My phone's been on all this time, but I'm just getting these messages now.*

Something was wrong. Dennis hoped that his phone had the problem, but he now feared that something was wrong with him.

"Can I get you anything, doctor?"

Dennis hid his shaking hands under his desk, resting them on his legs to help steady them. *Yes, you can get me something. But I don't know what that something is.*

"No. I'm okay, Deidre. You can go home."

She looked at him for a few moments, as though she was a practiced seer. "See you tomorrow, Doctor. Have a good evening."

"You, too, Deidre." In his confusion, Dennis had forgotten to thank her for her concern. He made a mental note to do that tomorrow.

Seven unaccounted-for hours. Dennis didn't remember a single second of those seven hours and nobody had seen him during that time. It was as if he had turned off his phone and hid from the world, like some men do when they go to a strip club in the middle of the day. Maybe that was it. Maybe he went to a strip club, got drunk or drugged, and didn't recall a thing. Only Dennis didn't know any strip clubs, had never been to a strip club before, and even if he had gone and gotten drunk, he would have remembered leaving the hospital to get there and back. Dennis took off his jacket and shirt and inspected his arms for tattoos. He pulled up his pants and lowered his socks to check his legs, as well. A tattoo was another reasonable—or crazy—explanation for those missing seven hours. But no tattoo. He would have liked a tattoo to have been the answer.

Dennis walked through a fog as he got ready to leave the office for home. He looked at his watch, his phone, his silver Seiko desk clock a dozen times—maybe more—but still couldn't make sense of what had just happened to him. Worse, he'd need to tell Rachel that he had a problem he couldn't fix. Surgeons don't like not being able to fix things.

During the elevator ride down, Dennis had an idea. He jabbed the button for the second floor just as the elevator approached that floor. He hoped it was a good idea.

"I want a rapid tox screen," Dennis instructed the phlebotomist as he walked into the hematology lab. Undoubtedly, she was going to be bewildered and possibly even concerned that a surgeon would suddenly ask for his own drug screening blood test, but Dennis didn't care. When the technician furled her eyebrows, Dennis repeated his request: "A rapid tox screen." Dennis read her ID badge. "Take my blood, Ms. Greenlee, and do it stat."

Every hospital has the ability to quickly test for a wide range of legal and illegal drugs. When an unresponsive patient who isn't a trauma victim is wheeled in the emergency room, being able to determine what drug that patient has in their system—and quickly—is all that stands between the living and that patient's parents attending a funeral. Mount Sinai Hospital's rapid tox screen tested for amphetamine, cannabinoids, cocaine, opiates, phencyclidine, barbiturates, and benzodiazepines. One of those might be the answer to the question that was now foremost in Dennis' mind.

"It'll take forty-five minutes to get the results," the phlebotomist said, as she closed the paperback novel she was holding. Something called *We're All Kings Now*.

"You can do it in five, so do it in five." Dennis' stony glare, devoid of all emotions save for apprehension and intimidation, clearly convinced her that she did not want to argue with this surgeon.

"Okay," Greenlee said. She opened blood kit, took out an alcohol packet, wiped his left arm, and, more mindfully than usual, inserted a needle into his vein.

The tests were negative for any commonly abused drugs. Dennis considered ordering more tests, including those that looked for infections, because bacteriological toxins could cause a variety of neurological conditions, but decided not to. An unnoticed infection with no known precipitator was about as likely as the strip club scenario. Dennis remembered reading in a journal how West Nile Virus could cause dementia—or had in one single case in Florida—but there was virtually no West Nile in New York, and in that case, the patient was elderly, probably with undiagnosed early onset dementia. *When you hear hoofbeats, think horses, not zebras.* He heard hoofbeats, but Dennis couldn't think of a single horse that would explain that day's and the previous night's missing hours.

Dennis arrived home about thirty minutes before Rachel. That gave him time to think about how to tell her what had happened, but all the time in the world wouldn't have helped him figure out a good way to explain things. There were no reasonable explanations—rather, no explanations at all—that made sense. People just don't disappear for hours and not remember anything, unless there's a serious neurological or pathological issue. When Rachel arrived, Dennis took her briefcase, rested it on the foyer floor, and kissed her even before she took off her coat.

"What's the matter?" Rachel asked.

"What do you mean?"

"Your kiss. It's—what's the way to put it?—flat. Those aren't your lips. Something's the matter."

Dennis looked into Rachel's eyes and nodded.

"Tell me about it," Rachel said, as she hung her coat in the closet and hooked her keys on the magnetic hanger on the door.

They talked about Dennis' fugue states while they drank red wine and ate moo shu pork. Rachel asked detailed, probing questions, most of which Dennis couldn't answer. He couldn't identify a trigger that sparked his disappearance. He couldn't find any evidence that he had gone anywhere—no ticket stubs, muddy shoes, receipts, or missing money. Rachel went online to see if there were any inexplicable charges to their joint Visa card, but there were none. They inspected Dennis' email account together, but that also offered no clues. Most baffling of all was Dennis' own watch, which was off by the same seven hours he couldn't account for.

Rachel was amused by Dennis' tattoo theory but less charmed by the strip club possibility. "If you land at a strip club for seven hours, you're going to need to rent a permanent room there." Rachel's face said that she was joking but then again not.

Dennis kissed her again. This time it felt better.

"What do you think happened, sweetie?"

"That's all I've been thinking about, and I have no idea," Dennis said. "Nothing makes sense. I don't feel ill. I don't have any other symptoms, at least not medical ones. I'm even feeling more energetic than usual, which is a good sign that there's not anything pathological in progress. I almost feel as if I've been breathing invigorating mountain air."

"Sec," Rachel said, looking relieved. She got up from the table, walked into the kitchen, and removed two containers of Häagen-Dazs sweet cream coffee caramel ice cream from the refrigerator. She brought the pint tubs to the table, spoons already in place, angling out from the ice cream containers like swords in stone. "Now you'll feel even better."

"I'm really glad I'm home. I don't know everything there is to know about the mind-body connection when it comes to healing, but my mind and body certainly feel better being close to your mind and body."

The Häagen-Dazs had fully worked its magic. Rachel's face relaxed, as a calmness replaced lines of concern that had stretched across her forehead. She took another spoonful of ice cream and said, "You're the doctor. What do you do next?"

"Next I see a neurologist. I'm going to give Bob Hastings a call first thing in the morning."

Rachel nodded. "I like Bob. I can't speak to his qualifications as a doctor, but he's a nice guy." Bob Hastings, Mount Sinai Hospital's head of neurology, and his wife, Ellen, were Dennis and Rachel's balcony friends. Twice a year Dennis and Rachel had them over for a cramped, Manhattan style barbecue of swordfish, grilled vegetables, and take out chocolate cake from Manny's Cakes. They cooked on the micro balcony but ate indoors because there was no way to squeeze four people and food onto the balcony. They joked that the barbecue was just an excuse to have the cake, but given how long the weekend lines at Manny's Cakes were, those desserts were nothing to joke about. Anticipating

Manny's cake while they were eating their salad and fish also gave them a pleasant alternative to discussing medicine, hospital administration, and malpractice insurance.

"Bob's great," Dennis agreed. "He'll probably be able to figure out what I've got in a Manhattan minute."

"He will." Rachel enclosed Dennis fingers with her hand. She could never entirely wrap her hand around his fingers, but she like the way they felt. "Don't worry, sweetheart. As you always tell your own patients, 'you're in good hands,' because you are."

"I'm not worried," Dennis said, raising his glass for another clink. He rarely did it, but Dennis hated lying to his wife.

# CHAPTER 2

## TOMORROW

"Where have you been?" Rachel asked, her face exchanging pale for crimson. The veins on her forehead expanded, and an emotion that Dennis couldn't yet decipher was bubbling under her skin. Rachel's hands rested on her hips, and her tensed arms formed two severe triangles.

Dennis propped himself up in bed. Rachel was already dressed, wearing a dark blue dress and black shoes. Dennis didn't recognize the dress. He also didn't recognize Rachel's new, shorter hair style and was confused by how her hair had changed overnight. Dennis stroked his chin as if to say, "I don't understand what you're talking about."

Dennis was fully clothed in bed, minus his jacket and tie, which he had taken off before dinner. His phone was still in his pocket. He was still wearing his shoes in bed, a forbidden activity in their house. *Rachel will be angry with me. I don't blame her.*

What he'd first thought was morning light—maybe he'd had too much wine during dinner and tumbled into bed without knowing it—was actually early evening. The last shadows of the sunset were just about gone. The moon, low on the horizon, peeked out through the canyon that was 63rd Street. It was the next day. *I've been in bed for nearly twenty-four hours.*

Dennis glanced around the room, noticing objects that were out of place, a little odd. There was a second framed photo of Dennis and Rachel on the bureau. The cellphone on the night table was thinner, with radically curved edges. The Oriental rug at the foot of their bed was more worn as if somebody wearing golf cleats had been pacing back and forth on it all night long.

Despite a profound sense of dislocation, Dennis physically felt fine. No hangover. Peppy, actually. He wasn't woozy, groggy, or in any kind of pain. He felt no trace of having been drunk, the one thing that would have explained Rachel's begrudging willingness to let him fall into bed with his shoes still on.

"I need to make that appointment with Bob. I'll call him now." Dennis propped himself up.

Rachel stood, still staring at him. She didn't say a word and, like a cat that's studying its owner, she didn't move.

"Hun?" Dennis asked.

"Where have you been?" Rachel repeated softly, her lips stiff. "Where have you been, Dennis?"

"I guess I fell asleep after dinner and slept through the entire day? I'm sorry that I got into bed with my shoes on. I'll change and wash the sheets. It's my fault." Dennis couldn't fathom how he'd got from dinner table to bed without remembering that, but there was no denying that he had. And no denying that he needed medical help, urgently. A freakish sickness was sucking him into deep, rocky earth, and soon the weight of the rocks would keep him from being able to climb up and out. Despite feeling good, he wasn't okay. He knew that, as sure as he knew when one of his patients was sick.

"You've been gone for two years," Rachel finally said.

"What are you talking about?" Dennis asked. "Don't be funny." Dennis sat up fully, his legs bent over the edge, feet firmly on the floor.

Rachel sat down next to Dennis. The mattress shifted slightly, like a wave that traveled across the ocean until it finally reached a beach, tired yet content that its destination had been found. She gave Dennis a hug, then put her hands on his shoulders and pushed herself back. "Dennis, it's June 4, 2019. I last saw you on April 14, 2017. That was more than two years ago."

"I can't believe that." Dennis took a deep breath and let it out slowly.

Rachel leaned over to the night table and picked up her phone. She blinked at the iris identification screen, and the phone lit up: Tuesday, June 4, 2019. Forecast: Sunny, 83 F, humidity 61%. Rachel picked up the television remote and clicked on the TV, which was already tuned into CNN. On the upper left-hand corner of the screen, Dennis read the words, "June 4, 2019, 7:26 PM."

Dennis put his hands in Rachel's. He kissed her. She retreated at first, but then kissed him back before breaking their embrace a few seconds later. She slid a couple of inches away from him, creating a small static discharge that snapped between her dress and the blanket.

*African trypanosomiasis? A brain tumor?* Neither made sense. Nothing made sense.

"Where have you been? Where do you go?" Rachel asked, her broken voice sad and angry.

Dennis shook his head. "I don't know what's happening to me. I don't know where I go."

"Two years, Dennis. You must know something. You couldn't have been in a coma in some far off place for two years." She paused. "Tell me. Whatever it is, wherever you have gone, I want to know."

"I swear I don't know. I need to see Bob Hastings."

"Bob? Bob died in January from a heart attack."

"Oh no," Dennis said. He could not dam in his grief.

Rachel let him cry. When Dennis stopped, he looked at her and could tell from her red, puffy eyes that she had cried every day for the past two years. "I'm sorry," Dennis said. "I don't know what's happening." There was no deceit in his eyes, only confusion and dolor.

Rachel hugged Dennis again. "Okay," she said. They sat together for many minutes, neither uttering a word. Dennis couldn't think of a single thing to say because he didn't understand what was going on. He had no vocabulary to describe the indescribable. There was nothing in his education, training, or experience that gave him even a scintilla of information that he could grasp onto for support. He was free falling fast through a bottomless black abyss.

Rachel saw a lost puppy in Dennis' face.

She summoned her executive mode, something she never did at home. Rachel had always been scrupulous about keeping work out of their home life. She talked about work—including complaining about it from time to time—of course, but her work persona never encroached on their personal space. Dennis joked that Rachel had two personalities—her home personality, affectionate, smart, sensual, sweet, and her work personality, which Dennis simply referred to as her "mysterious evil twin". Rachel's early years as an architect had been devoted almost exclusively to designing things. It didn't matter if it was a school auditorium, kids' bedroom, or a skyscraper with a helipad on top, she was driven to make newness. Now, as a full partner, Rachel spent more time as a manager than a designer, where she had to make tough, risky, and sometimes antagonistic decisions. But she found that she liked solving crises. Today, she was going to solve the gravest crisis she had ever faced. Her lips stopped quivering. Her eyes narrowed. She stood up, grabbed Dennis' hand, and pulled him up and off the bed. "Let's go."

"Go where?"

"To Mount Sinai. We're going to get you wired and tubed up. Tested. X-rayed, MRIed, CT scanned, and everything else that the hospital can do."

"But it's late. And I don't have a referring physician."

"Yeah, but you used to be a surgeon there, so that won't be a problem."

*Used to be.*

The tests started the following morning. Dennis began to understand that it wasn't the tests themselves that were the main unpleasant, uncomfortable, or painful (though some were) part of being in the hospital. It was the interminable waiting that drove patients crazy. Not just waiting for a turn to ride the frosty X-ray table, but waiting for tests to stop after they had started. Dennis couldn't count the number of times he had to hold his breath for what seemed like a marathon underwater swim—waiting inside waiting. But the waiting would be worth it if the answer to what had been causing his disappearances and memory loss resided inside one of the multimillion dollar machines.

Distractions by way of books and movies served Dennis well during his three days in the hospital. He knew that chances were high that one of the exhaustive tests would find something wrong—a spot on his kidneys, a shadow adjacent to his spine, a blood value that was outside the normal range—something that would rev up his internal anxiety machine. Or a dot in his brain that should not be there, but which could explain his disappearances and memory loss. He knew that not every spot or abnormal reading was destined to become a killer, or inescapable, but if an anomaly were found, often an Ouija board or a coin toss are as good as a medical degree for deciding what should be done. "We could operate and put you on chemo, but you could also live for fifty years with that lesion. We don't have any way of knowing which is best." Dennis had said similar words to patients.

Every moment spent reading books or watching movies was a moment not spent imagining what incurable horror might be growing inside him. So he read and watched a lot.

And yet, more than anything Dennis wanted to know.

"Hello, Dr. Tanner," the young physician said as she walked into Dennis' newly renovated room. Many hospitals, including Mount Sinai, had transformed their scrofulous chambers into calmer, prettier places that actually helped patients recover. (And raised room prices to go along with the improvements.) Mount Sinai had redecorated many of its rooms with art that drew patients' attention away from anxiety-fomenting blood pressure readers, oxygen spigots, and syringe bins. The painting of Iceland's Gullfoss Falls, wide couch, flat screen television, and desk, made Dennis' room look more like a Hilton than a hospital room in 'House.'

The young physician put her clipboard down on the desk. "I'm Dr. Kenny." She extended her hand. "It's good to meet you."

Dennis couldn't stop his mind from wandering to the thought that every patient has when they're visited by a resident: *Did my doctor just graduate high school?* Dennis also wondered, *Did patients once think that about me? Probably.* Despite her youth, he was grateful—and anxious about what news she had. He didn't mind young doctors because residents brought with them a vigor and inquisitiveness that more seasoned doctors no longer had, and that could be a plus for patients.

"I have good news," Dr. Kenny said. "There's nothing notably wrong with you. No toxins, no cancers, no growths, no infections, no systemic abnormal blood numbers. All your organ functions are within normal ranges."

"I guess that's good news. I'm glad that I'm not going to die soon." He really meant that. A bona fide sea of relief rushed over him. "But I was hoping that some test would reveal why I have long gaps in my memory and why I disappear for extended periods of time."

Dr. Kenny pulled the desk chair close to the bed and sat down. "Well, we did find that you have increased levels of chromium and cobalt in your blood."

"What does that mean?"

Dr. Kenny looked down at the manila folder in her lap, flipped a few pages, and read out loud, "Cobalt concentrations ranged between 0.8 and 3.3 μg/L in blood and between 0.4 and 5.1 μg/L in serum. Mean chromium concentrations ranged between 1.4 and 2.1 μg/L in blood and between 1.5 and 5.1 μg/L in serum."

"I'm a little lost. I'm a surgeon, not a hematologist."

"These are the kind of cobalt and chromium levels that we sometimes see after metal-on-metal hip replacements. Occasionally, metal leaches into the blood, raising the cobalt and chromium levels. But you don't have any implants, so it's all a little curious."

"Curious?"

"Yes. Your cobalt and chromium levels aren't dangerous or anything to worry about, but they're not associated with anything other than hip replacements."

"Do you think that these could be causing my fugue states?"

"I don't see how. I consulted with a neurologist, Dr. Peter Mann, who said that there's nothing in the literature about high cobalt or chromium levels causing neurological problems."

Dennis had heard of Peter Mann, though he'd never met him. Dr. Mann was well regarded.

"What's your best guess? I'll accept that because it's better than no guess at all."

"Best guess?" Dr. Kenny repeated. She took in a deep breath and exhaled slowly. "It's an unknown. Like HIV or prions were until we found them. Or like the central nervous system lymphatic vessels, which were discovered just two years ago."

Dennis had heard about the central nervous system lymphatic vessels, which move the brain's lymphatic fluid to adjacent lymph nodes

Kenny added, "There's still a lot we don't know about the human body and medicine."

"It's refreshing to hear a doctor say that."

"I'd only say it to another doctor," Kenny said with a sly smile. "But whatever you have, there's no damage being done to any of your organs or cells."

"So what do we do now?"

"Now you go home," Dr. Kenny said, looking around the room. "Unless you'd like to order from room service again."

"No, thank you." Hospital rooms may have improved, but hospital food still made high school cafeteria food taste like a four-star restaurant.

"I'll get your discharge papers moving. You'll be out of here within the hour."

Disappointed, but not defeated, Dennis changed from his pajamas into his street clothes. He placed two phone calls: one to Dr. Mann's office to schedule an appointment, and one, reluctantly but sensibly, to Dr. Jason Stern's office. Dr. Stern was a psychiatrist with whom Dennis had consulted about a few patients. He liked Stern, the least judgmental person he knew. As he packed his clothes, books, iPad, and toiletries, Dennis examined the room, as if there might be some clue hiding behind the TV or lurking under the desk. His life had become a mystery; his hospital room was as good a place to search for clues as anywhere else.

There were no clues.

Dennis told the orderly that he didn't need a wheelchair. To hell with the hospital tradition of wheeling every patient to the front door. It was an antiquated custom that Dennis wanted nothing to do with. The orderly asked if he had made arrangements for anyone to pick him up. "No. I haven't been sedated. I don't have any broken bones or post-op condition."

The orderly looked upset.

"I shouldn't have snapped at you," Dennis said. "I'm just stressed."

"No worries. Hospitals do that," the orderly replied with certainty. "Don't I know it."

"I'll take a cab and will be fine. Thank you."

Dennis was surprised to smell beef cooking, a savory salty-sweet aroma, when he opened his apartment door. At one in the afternoon, Rachel should be in the thick of the office, managing projects, designing buildings, putting out fires. But she was home. Unexpected, but Dennis was happy that she had decided to take the day off. He hadn't called Rachel from the hospital because he wanted to surprise her, but the surprise was on him.

When the apartment door squeaked opened, Rachel called out, "Who's there?" Dennis heard his wife's voice, but not her voice. The voice was like a dirt road in August, sun-dried, cracked, and uneven. "Who's there? Rachel repeated.

"It's me, sweetheart. They released me from the hospital. Let me hang up my coat and I'll be right there."

"Dennis?" Rachel called. "Is that you, Dennis?"

An old woman came to the door. Dennis dropped his overnight bag. His mouth hung open. "Rachel?" Before him stood his wife. Her once long, blonde hair was now brittle, gray, and short. Her wrinkled face was tinged orange, her body three inches shorter. Her legs wobbled. It was as if Rachel had walked through an aging machine.

Dennis knew what had happened, and he could tell from Rachel's expression, the way her sorrowful eyes fixed on him, that she knew, too. "It's 2062, Dennis. It's July 8th, 2062. I'm..." Rachel couldn't complete her sentence.

"I'm sorry," was all Dennis could say. He hugged her and wanted to hold her for as long as the universe would allow.

"Why are you doing this to us?" Dennis shouted at the ceiling. "Who the fuck are you that you can torture and rob us?" Dennis shot his fist toward the ceiling. "You have no right!"

"It's okay, sweetheart. Long ago, I accepted our fate. Don't be angry about it."

"I still don't know where I go. At the hospital—I guess that was thirty-five years ago now but also just an hour ago—they found nothing wrong with me. Just some metal levels out of balance, but nothing that would explain what's happening. When I left our apartment three days ago, things were just a little wrong, but now they're raging mad. I'm angry. And I'm scared. What's happening?"

Rachel put her hands on Dennis shoulders. "I never expected to see you again. You checked out of Mount Sinai and then vanished. But this time it wasn't days or months, it was for decades. In the beginning, I called the hospital every day. I called the police, the FBI, our friends, your family. Nobody knew where you were. But after a time, I knew. There could only be one explanation."

Rachel's eyes moistened. "I thought I had lost you forever. I missed you desperately." She managed a small smile. "But I'm glad to see you before I die."

"Don't say that. I'm sure that in 2062 people live for a very long time."

"I'm sure that some do," Rachel said. "But I have liver cancer. There's still no cure. It's spread to my pancreas and bones—stage M4. I've got a couple of months at most. But you know that. You're a surgeon."

"Let's lie down," Dennis suggested. *I want to carry you in the future with me, holding hands as this capricious wind blows us through time. We'll travel together into the years and decades until we find a cure. I won't let you go.*

"Yes. I'll turn down the oven, and we can do that."

"Do you remember when we were dating and you switched your apartment door Halloween decorations?" Rachel asked after they settled into bed.

"I do. I don't think I've ever laughed that hard."

"Me neither," Rachel said.

They held hands as Rachel recounted how she had admired the decoration on Dennis' apartment door, a black cat in an orange witch's hat. The cute decoration was one of the many things that had endeared her to Dennis. He had a soft spot. How many single guys in their thirties put Halloween decorations of cats, or decorations at all, on their doors?

Halloween came and went, but Dennis kept the decoration on his door beyond October 31. Past the first week into November, past the second week, too, well after most trick or treating children had consumed their last Snickers bar and all that remained were green lollipops.

Rachel had teased Dennis, wondering if the only animal he could take care of was a miniature cat decoration, and suggesting that at this rate he might as well keep the Halloween cat on his door because next Halloween was a mere eleven months away.

On those nights that they had slept apart, which had become few and fewer, Dennis escorted Rachel to the subway, a brisk five-minute walk from his apartment. One evening, Rachel forgot her cell phone at Dennis' apartment. She couldn't call him to let him know that she was coming back, so she would just pop back in—she had her own key. But on the way back from seeing her off at the 79th and Lexington subway station, Dennis had bought a Thanksgiving decoration for his apartment at the supermarket around the corner and substituted his bewitching cat for a turkey surrounded by a cornucopia of fall foods.

When Rachel arrived back at Dennis' apartment just a minute after he'd changed decorations, she was baffled, unsure about whether she remembered the apartment Rachel had been in hundreds of time before, and unsure if she was in the right place. Actually, she was pretty certain that she was in the wrong place. The decoration wasn't Dennis'. Rachel checked the apartment number, 12D, twice, three times, until she was finally bold enough to try her key and walk into what might be somebody else's apartment. *The strange sorcerer cat had done something.* But it was Dennis who had been the unforeseen magician that night.

They laughed nonstop for minutes, pausing only to gasp at air and wipe away their gushing laughter tears.

"That was the funniest moment in my life," Rachel said as she squeezed Dennis' hand as hard as her ancient muscles would let her. "Of all the nights to change the decoration you refused to change, you picked the one time I forgot my phone and had to come back without calling you."

"It was so unexpected and hysterical. You were totally surprised. I was, too."

As they lay together, Rachel unfastened her necklace, four concentric gold circles with a peridot radiating from the middle. She uncurled Dennis' fingers, put the necklace in his palm, and then wrapped his fingers around it.

"What's this for?" Dennis asked. The necklace carried her warmth.

"This was the first present you ever gave me. Take it to remember me always. Wherever you go, I will be with you."

A powerful morning sun penetrated Dennis' eyelids, an iri-sation of red and yellow that yanked him out of his sleep. He blinked a few times and sat up. Rachel wasn't there. And this wasn't his bed. Or his bedroom.

Dennis hoisted himself upright and went to the window. He needed orientation, an anchor of any kind. *Where am I?* In his peripheral vision, he saw a flock of par-rots south above Second Avenue, a blur of green, red, yellow in the corner of his eye. *Parrots?* The Manhattan view he had known for the past eight years was still there. The deco apartment building with its magical interplay of glass, brick, and bronze relief was unchanged. The ten-storey apartment building with the fire escapes that always struck Dennis as more fragile than a paper flower in the rain stood as it always had, red brick holding the fire escape securely in place. Like a navigator looking at the stars for his bearing, Dennis was reassured by the buildings that he was where he thought he was and wanted to be. But his bedroom wasn't his bedroom. The general size and configuration of the walls and doors were about right, but only that was familiar. Large flat panels covered most of the walls. The casement windows were clear sheets of uninterrupted glass without window panes. And clean—something that Dennis and Rachel had never gotten around to doing. The bed was lower to the ground than his had been and rested on cylinders about the thickness of a sink's drain pipe. The carpeting was—Dennis didn't know how to describe it, so he took his socks off and felt it—a thin but plush-feeling material that warmed his feet but wasn't warm itself. His bureau, night table—everything—were gone and had been replaced with furniture made from what looked like a silver, plasticky material. The end table photos of Dennis and Rachel were gone, too, replaced by a digital photo of woman in her forties with auburn hair, standing in front of a mountain with a serrated, snow covered top.

Dennis circled around the room like a child who walks through an amusement park's mirror maze designed to make you accept a fate of being lost forever. He didn't expect to be able to find his way out, but there was nothing else to do but try.

"Rachel!" Dennis shouted. "Rachel!" He didn't expect that she could answer, but he called to her anyway, hoping that his voice would reach out to her through time.

Heavy footsteps pounded toward the room before the door burst open. "Who are you?" a tall man, about fifty with a long jaw and thick eyebrows, yelled at Dennis. He was dressed in black pants and a black shirt that was buttoned all the way to his neck. "What are you doing in my apartment?" The man held an iron in his right hand. It looked funny, but Dennis knew exactly what kind of damage a heavy, metal object like that could do to his head. "Get the hell out of here before I call the 911s or beat you to a pulp."

Dennis put his hands in the air to show submission. "I'm going." He gingerly bent down for his socks and shoes but didn't put them on because he figured that the muscular man with the iron wasn't going to tolerate any delay in his exit. Dennis backed up, walking slowly and smoothly as one might when confronted with a growling dog, bared teeth seeking meat.

As he carefully walked backwards he noticed other changes in his apartment. The walls had a luminescent coating. There were no stand-alone lights anywhere, just walls that glowed. As Dennis was herded toward the front door, the walls he passed by glowed brighter and the walls he moved away from became dimmer. Almost every wall had a large flat-screen on it. The screen in the hallway displayed a perfect reproduction of Claude Monet's 'Haystacks'; one of the screens in the living room showed Édouard Manet's 'The

Railway'. He didn't say a word and certainly wasn't going to ask the man about his Monet-Manet fandom. He glanced into the kitchen as he passed it; the refrigerator's exterior metamorphosed from opaque to transparent and then back to opaque. Cheeses, sandwiches, hot dogs, eggs, and yogurts in the man's refrigerator made Dennis realize that he was hungry. His hunger would have to wait.

Several small, silent drones about the size of a thumb hovered around the ceiling. Dennis had no idea what they were for.

A gray and white tabby cat rubbed against Dennis' leg and spoke a subdued meow. The man looked at his cat and then at Dennis with a threatening expression that said, "Don't even think about it." He raised the iron a little higher.

As Dennis crossed the transom, still in reverse, he stopped for a moment. His heart was racing. He wondered if his pupils were dilated. "What year is this?" he asked breathlessly, hoping that the man wouldn't think he was too insane to answer.

"It's 2112."

The man slammed the door with such ferociousness that the hallway's dust was lifted in the air. It swirled around Dennis' legs like the kind of leaf storm you see on autumn days, controlled by an invisible whirlwind. Dennis heard the locks to his apartment engage and felt the finality of a life lost. Everything he had been was now behind that locked door.

*Ninety-five years. It's been ninety-five years since this madness began.* Dennis didn't know where to go. He opened his hands and looked at his palms, as though he were a palm reader, hoping to understand his future, to know his path. His palms were imprinted with long lines, short lines, and branches growing in divergent directions, a forest that hides its true intentions. Occult knowledge did not come to Dennis; his palms stayed silent. He didn't know what to do. He knew not a soul in this world. He was alone with nobody to turn to, nobody to call, nobody who would believe him. *Where do I even begin?*

He wanted to light a candle for Rachel. He wanted answers. He wanted peace.

Dennis sat on the staircase landing of his—what had been their—eighteenth-floor apartment. *I will find Rachel's grave and visit her. Maybe I should start taking one of the psychotropic drugs I once imagined to be the cause of all of this,* he thought. *That might send me back to my time.* But he knew that it would not.

As he sat, Dennis was touched by the joyous memory of their first kiss. He was in medical school at Brown, while Rachel was getting her master's in architecture. They had both been studying late and had parked themselves at Blue State Coffee, near the campus, for a change of scenery and to keep caffeine coursing through their blood. Exam week was around the corner and caffeine was nearly as important as oxygen.

Dennis and Rachel, still strangers to each other, were sitting at the same table at Blue State. Then 10:00 p.m. came, and exam week or not, that was the coffee shop's closing time. They let out simultaneous yawns when the unsympathetic barista unceremoniously cut off their caffeine supply. Their yawns were wide and long, like a lion in a circus who opens its mouth to let in the lion tamer's head. They laughed with each other, and then Rachel asked, "Do you want to get some coffee somewhere?"

"Sure," Dennis said. "I'm going to need it tonight."

The only problem was that Providence, Rhode Island, wasn't New York, and when ten p.m. butted into their lives, the choices were three: 7-Eleven, Rachel's apartment, or Dennis' apartment. The only seating at the nearby 7-Eleven was the sidewalk curb, so they opted for Rachel's apartment, where they drank coffee and studied together until

6:00 a.m. Rachel and Dennis smiled and stole glances at each other all night long. And they drank a lot of coffee. Periodically, they'd surface from their textbooks and talk for a few minutes—sometimes about medicine or architecture, but mostly about the kind of doctor and architect they each wanted to be.

When it was time for Dennis to leave, Rachel walked him to the staircase of her three-storey walk-up. To this day Dennis wasn't sure if it was because of the Grand Canyon quantity of coffee, with its myriad complex, organic molecules, or the lack of sleep, or something else, but before he turned to say goodbye, he kissed her. It wasn't even a date, and he kissed her. Not on the cheek, either, but on the lips—a soft and full kiss. Rachel let his lips linger and took his hand in hers.

That was a long time ago, but he could still feel that kiss.

Dennis was on the verge of surrendering to this nameless phenomena. He didn't comprehend the why or how of this phenomenon, but there could be no doubt—almost no doubt—about the what. He was traveling through time, a victim of a force that would have been unbelievable except for the fact that there were no plausible, alternative explanations. Something inexplicable and powerful, something out of his control and beyond his imagination, was propelling Dennis into the future. Time traveler. It wasn't exotic, exciting, or amazing. It was meaningless.

He heard zebras.

He sat on the cold, cement stairwell, dimly lit because, in every century, staircases were designed to dissuade use through darkness. A tenebrous space that herded him in one direction: down. Dennis imagined the first-floor staircase door opening to a bleak world where sunshine had failed and where he would fade like slow-dying plants in an endless winter. He saw saturnine clouds swirling above him, a vortex of gray and black pulling in all matter—cars, streetlights, sidewalks, buildings. He saw a dark, rumbling nebula consuming light, and with it, hope. Dennis needed a plan. Without one he might continue traveling, like boats of a thousand years ago, pushed to the very edge of the Earth and then over that edge to where the monsters lived. Without a plan, he would find out what happens to the universe at the end of time itself—knowledge that comes with a terrible price.

What does a stranger do in a strange land? Where can you go when you have no friends, money, or even an understanding of where you are? A church, yes, that was one place that welcomed strangers, but Dennis doubted that the cause of his leaps was theological, or the cure spiritual. He had prayed from time to time but knew that he needed an antidote stronger than prayer. The library was another possibility, but what were the chances that he'd find the answer in a book? He could ask a librarian about time travel. Librarians were undoubtedly used to hearing all sorts of crazy people with crazy ideas, and Dennis didn't want to be counted among the crazies, and the possibility remained that he was indeed one of those crazy people who are certain that they'd seen the smooth metal insides of spaceships. Besides, he could spend years at the library with nothing to show for it. The police? No way. A Starbucks, assuming that they existed in 2112? Maybe. Perhaps he'd have a serendipitous encounter with a fellow time traveler. Eddies and currents and ripples and waves in time might just bring two time travelers together. The idea of an outlander saddling into the seat beside him, giving Dennis a knowing look, and saying, "I'm a time traveler, too" was as appealing as it was unrealistic.

*What other place can somebody just walk into?*

A hospital! *I could go back to Mount Sinai Hospital. There would be records of my having been both a doctor and patient. I'd be a walking, breathing puzzle that somebody would have to solve. My DNA's on file, and comparing the file with the living, breathing me would be undisputable proof that something extraordinary is happening. A man born in 1977, but who still looks like he's forty when he should be 135. Either I'm not aging, which is impossible, or I'm a time traveler, which is slightly less impossible.* Dennis knew how doctors reasoned and believed that somebody would think along these lines. It might take a while; doctors aren't inclined to think zebras until they've eliminated all the horses. *In 2112, somebody might able to figure this out.*

*I might even make a friend.*

*And I'd have a bed and food.*

The idea of a team of physicians from an array of specialties working together to study and eventually solve the riddle of the world's first time traveler was the first happy thought Dennis had since this all had begun. He could hear Rachel whispering in his ear as her soft hair tickled his neck: "Do this. Go back to Mount Sinai. Find the answers for us." Rachel would be pleased that specialists from nuclear medicine to genetics to hematology to neurology would focus their collective brilliance on him. She would want him to discover what was happening and to make it stop. Dennis reached into his pocket and wrapped his fingers around Rachel's necklace, the cool metal warmed by his hand and Rachel's memory. *I will find the answer for you, my love. I promise.*

Dennis walked down the eighteen flights, the building's thrum filling his ears. The walk gave him time to think about how he would introduce himself at Mount Sinai Hospital. That could be tricky. "Hello, I'm a time traveler" would get him an appointment with a psychiatrist, assuming that he wasn't first escorted out by two burly guys with "Mount Sinai Security" embroidered on their jackets. "I'm 135 years old" would do the same thing. First impressions are as important in medicine as they are in business and dating, and this wasn't an easy first impression to devise. Then it hit him.

*I'll present myself as a cardiac patient. Chest pain, shortness of breath, dizziness—classic symptoms of a cardiac event. They'll run tests, including looking at DNA markers for heart disease. I'll suggest taking a look at the medical records of Dr. Dennis Tanner, whom I'll say is my grandfather. When they see that my "grandfather's" DNA and my DNA are identical, that will start the ball rolling. Only identical twins have the same DNA; parents, grandparents, and other ancestors won't.*

*A medical mystery in search of a solution. The dream of every doctor.*

# CHAPTER 3
## SOMEWHERE

Dennis gave himself a thumbs up as he stepped out of his old apartment building. He took a deep, hopeful breath. He exited into an unwelcome, alien world.

The perspective that Dennis had used to orient himself from the eighteenth floor of his apartment building was gone. The building next door, and the next, and the one after that weren't just missing their fire escapes—they were themselves missing. Towering metal and glass monoliths rose where brownstones and storefronts had once stood. Shiny, some curved, some sharply angular, some twisted, and all touching the clouds. Sunlight took a sinuous route around these buildings as if the buildings themselves could bend light. Underfoot, the pavement felt rubbery; gone was the hard cement that had always been beneath his shoes. Red egg-shaped objects flew above, following the avenues and streets at about fifty-storey height. Several large, oddly shaped aircraft, with four sets of wings angling out in different directions and themselves surrounded by a torus, massive in size, hovered in place well above even the tallest buildings. Dennis couldn't even begin to guess their purpose. He spun around. His old apartment building was gone, too, and in its place was another super-skyscraper, towering hundreds of stories into the sky. Dennis stood, stared, and wondered. *Where am I? New York City. It's always New York.*

*But when am I?*

Was the building where his apartment had been a residence, an office, or something else? The building looked like a twisted slide, steep and smooth, as if somebody could ride the exterior all the way down. It had a rectangular core with a corkscrew exterior. Several people came in and out, wearing what Dennis guessed weren't work clothes—nothing resembled a suit or uniform. The building was probably still an apartment building. Not that that would do him any good. He couldn't ring a bell, say he's a neighbor, and ask to crash on a couch for the night. Or even borrow a banana or yogurt. Dennis was homeless. Lost. And useless: his surgical skills undoubtedly as out of date here—whenever here was—as a doctor from 1700 would have been in 2017. Dennis was a relic.

*How am I supposed to eat? Where am I supposed to sleep?* Dennis felt sorry for himself for those and a thousand other reasons he couldn't articulate. He missed Rachel. He missed his work. He missed his friends. He missed his century and even all the chaos and anxieties that went with it.

Should haves. Life's regrets have a way of sneaking up on you, but Dennis' regrets encircled him all at once, like an army that had been hiding behind forest trees. *I should have taken more vacations with Rachel. I should have learned tennis or water skiing. I should have made more friends and spent more time with them. Rachel and I should have had children. Then I might have somebody here, a great-great-great grandchild—somebody.*

Dennis tried not to think about his regrets, which were pulling him deeper into a  psychogenic quicksand, but what could he do? He felt powerless because that was exactly what he was.

"Excuse me," Dennis said to a passerby. "Could you tell me what year this is?" There was no sense in hesitating or worrying about being embarrassed. Dennis was beyond embarrassment and didn't care what anyone thought about him. He wanted to know, *needed* to know. The woman, who looked about thirty, had short blonde hair and a face that had collected genes from Asia or a Native American or some distance place. She was about 5' 5" tall and wore tan, low-cut boots, jeans, and a light blue button-down shirt that didn't seem too different from clothing in his time. She gave Dennis a cursory once-over before answering. "It's 2300. Happy New Year."

"Thank you."

"You're welcome."

*2300. Oh, my god. What do I do?* Dennis looked to the sky again, his neck stretched so he could see the air above the rooftops. *Why are you doing this to me? Please, please stop.*

Dennis stood there, looked at the woman, and then gaped more at the buildings. They reminded Dennis of photos he'd seen of Dubai, except that in this place, in this New York of 2300, every building was tall, taller than anything that had existed in his time. Dennis swiveled his head up and down, mouth agape, pupils widely dilated, like he was on an African safari surrounded by all the animals at once, or was waking up to Antarctica's blue diamond icebergs after a night-time voyage.

Dennis started to walk away from the woman, but she called him back before he had strolled more than a few feet. "Hey. Is that a watch?"

"This?" Dennis asked as he lifted his wrist and showed the woman his watch close up.

"Yes. I've seen those in imageglyphs, but I've never seen one for real. I didn't even know that they're made anymore. Did you buy it new or is it an antique?

"It was a gift. It's from a long time ago."

"Does it work?"

Dennis stepped closer to this stranger. "Yes, it works great. It's the only thing I can count on. I wear it all the time."

"Cool. How does a watch work?"

It didn't take much imagination to understand that three centuries from now—from when his now had been—the art of analog time telling would be as arcane and perplexing as using an abacus was in 2017.

"I'm Dennis."

"Leah," she as she bowed slightly. "Nice to meet you."

"Here, let me show you how a watch works."

There was something comforting about teaching a person from the future about the past. There was something comforting, too, about sharing his most prized possession with another human being. Dennis pointed to the big hand, then the little hand, the second hand and explained the art of telling time. Periodically, he'd look at Leah's face to see if she was absorbing this new skill or if her face looked like she was swimming in deep water. Leah beamed at Dennis, and he knew that she wasn't just understanding this ancient skill, but enjoying it, too.

She asked a few questions during Dennis' lesson and then nodded. "Thanks. I now know how a watch works."

"You're welcome. I hope you can find a watch somewhere. They're functional works of art you can wear and enjoy."

"I want one. Hey, I'm free with nothing to do this afternoon. You look like you're free, too. Would you like to get a drink?"

*More conversation with somebody who's not trying to kill me. I could go for that.* "Sure. I could use a drink." *You have no idea how much I could use a drink.*

"My job's 50 human, 50 machine. Today's the machine's workday. Gotta find some way to fill the free. I have all day, but we'll drink slowly so that we don't overhooch and can remember what we talk about," she said with an agreeable laugh.

There was something unusual about New York other than the enormous, enigmatic buildings, elastic sidewalk, and flying objects in the sky. Dennis and the woman walked while he tried to put his finger on the peculiar problem that buzzed in his brain like a persistent mosquito. And then it hit him: there were no cars. New York City was without cars. A city without cars was a pasture, an oasis of quiet. New York may not have been this tranquil since before horses had walked on cobblestone streets, nearly 600 years in the past. Dennis liked it.

Running through the middle of the wide street that had once been Second Avenue was a canal about twenty feet wide. Or at least that was the closest analogy Dennis could come up with. Iridescent indigo water, bluer than any cloudless sky or sapphire that he had ever seen, spanned the center of the street. The perfectly placid water came right up to the edge of the street, like an endless pool, neither spilling over into the sidewalk or retreating from it. Leah walked swiftly.

*A fast walker, a New Yorker in any era.*

"Where are you from, Dennis?"

"Let's have that drink first, and I'll tell you."

"Sure," Leah said. "I like this day. If I'm required to take a day off, I'm happy that there's no snow. What about you? Are you a warm-weather lover or one of those adventure types who prefers skiing at the poles?"

"I'll take calm, comfortable, and warm," Dennis replied. His thoughts drifted back to his honeymoon in the Bahamas where he had been enveloped by the warm Caribbean and his wife's embrace all day, every day. They had joked about whether the Bahamas needed doctors and architects, and whether they could turn their seven-day honeymoon into seventy years. They talked about it after their honeymoon, too; staying forever on a warm tropical island was not on Dennis and Rachel's impossible list. One day they would.

"Yeah, me too."

Dennis and Leah walked along another block that was occupied by a single, towering edifice made of glass, metal, and something that looked like a brick with copper-colored glitter. Leah stopped. "Here's my favorite bar. I hope you like it." Leah took Dennis' hand and skipped a step forward to the building.

From the outside, the door looked like it led to another apartment building. There was no sign, no logo. Just an oval door that whooshed open, its two halves disappearing entirely into the sides of the frame, just as their noses were about crash into it. But it was a bar, all right. Dark, busy, thick with the smell of hops and barley. There was a hum of voices that spoke every possible syllable at the same time, a din that transformed English into something ancient and undecipherable.

Dennis tasted alcohol in the air. He thought that the bar was too busy for a weekday, but he wasn't even sure what day it was or even if weekdays mattered anymore. The bar used the same wall-glow lighting he had seen two centuries ago in his old apartment. Maybe that was still state of the art or perhaps this bar sported a retro look. The drinking glasses were familiar, some wide and squat, some tall and thin, like in his era, but the liquor bottles—vintage from his time, from before he was born, and probably from after he would have died—were for show. Colorful bottles lit from behind, glowed and beckoned. When somebody asked for a drink, the bartender put a glass into a small compartment, waited a few seconds, and then took out a glass filled with liquor.

"Welcome to Locomotive East," Leah said. "First time here?"

"Yes," Dennis said. He looked down as a small, dog-shaped robot circled the table. The dog robot's tongue lapped up a small puddle of spilled drink and circled their table once more before skittering off to another spot. Dennis wondered if it was programmed to get drunk from licking so many spilled drinks.

Leah, still holding Dennis' hand, said, "Sit here. I'm buying. It's a tradition that those who are free do the buying." Good, because Dennis didn't know if the dollars that he carried in his wallet would be worthless in 2300, worth a fortune to a collector, or land him in jail.

"Is it?"

"No, but you look like you're in need of something, so a drink is a good place to start."

"You're perceptive."

"Not perceptive enough to know what you'd like to whet your whistle."

"That'll be a whiskey, neat."

"Whiskey?"

*The future. Not everything is better.*

"Something I used to drink when I really needed one. What would you recommend?"

"I'll get us beers."

Dennis looked around as Leah got their drinks. Nobody was drinking alone, which struck Dennis as odd. In his time, there were always people drinking—or at least sitting and reading—alone, but this bar was populated exclusively by groups of two or more. Some customers were eating Day-Glo-colored foods—cherry red, coral blue, apple green—in unusual shapes: donuts, parallelograms, stars, hexagons, and what looked like a bead and ball necklace. Meticulous geometry ruled the food's design in this place. Dennis tried not to stare, but he was curious about what his next meal might be like, assuming he was here long enough to have one. He wondered if this bar's food was as different from home-cooked meals in 2300 as bar food had been in 2017. If he had been a time traveler from 1900 and landed in a bar in 2017, would he have assumed that people ate chicken wings, onion rings, and chili fries at home for dinner? That batter-fried fish was a universal staple? Maybe. Nobody's mindset is prepared for time travel.

Lean returned with their drinks. "So, where are you from?" she asked again. "Answering my questions is the price you have to pay for your drink."

Dennis downed almost the entire beer. He took his time responding, because no matter how he composed the answer in his head, it sounded lame to his mind's ear. So he just spit it out: "I am from New York, from the year 2017."

"I see." Leah's expression didn't change.

*I'm telling an unbelievable truth to a complete stranger.*

*I'm at a bar in the year 2300 having a drink with a complete stranger. Yesterday, I was in 2017 preparing a patient for surgery.*

"You don't have to believe me. I wouldn't believe me. And it doesn't matter if you believe me or not. I'm traveling into the future in fits and starts, and I don't know why. I don't know when it will stop, either. When I went to work one recent morning, my wife was thirty-five. The next time I saw her, she was seventy, and then she died. I didn't even get to say goodbye." Dennis added, "That's the truth."

"That's sad. It's sad when people you care for die," Leah said. Through her eyes, Dennis saw a hurt inside Leah's heart. She took a sip of her beer. "I'm not saying that I disbelieve you. You have an honest face. You can tell me your story."

"Look," Dennis said, as he took his wallet out of his back pocket. "Here's my driver's license." Dennis handed his license to Leah.

Leah lifted her left eyebrow.

"It's a government ID."

"Do you work for Us?"

"No. I'm a doctor. This is something that everyone has so that they can drive a car." Leah tilted her head slightly as if that would help her understand better. Dennis paused and reframed his words. "So that the government knows who you are. Here. It has my picture and my birthday, 1977. I was born on November 1, 1977."

Dennis pulled out his hospital ID. "Here's my identification for the hospital I work at. Worked at. It's the same me, same birthday."

"Odd cards, and your height and weight are in old American scale." Leah examined the pictures and the cards, puzzling over what they said, and then studied Dennis' face. "That is you. I don't think you're a wacko, but I'm going to withhold belief for a while longer." She took a long drink of her beer and then pushed the empty glass to the side. "That's a pretty tall tale, Dennis."

"I know. But I also know that it's happening, and there's nothing that I can do about it. Without warning, I'm scooped up by some invisible energy, force, machine, time warp, wormhole, black hole—I don't know what—and sent hours, years, or centuries into the future. The distance that I travel into the future changes each time. Insane, isn't it?"

Leah let Dennis fill in the narrative of who he had once been and where he had traveled over the past 300 years. He mostly talked about his work and the New York City he had lived in. Leah liked the descriptions of New York in the early 21st century and peppered Dennis with questions about transportation, the Empire State Building—which had been dismantled 125 years before—about crime, what Fifth Avenue was like, who ran the city, how garbage got collected, what brownstone buildings looked like, festivals and holidays, restaurants, what New Yorkers did in their free time, and more. Leah was especially curious about neighborhoods because history had consumed them over the centuries and replaced them with an efficient but boring homogeneity. In the course of their conversation, Dennis changed careers from physician to historian as he painted a world that was as alien to Leah as her time was to him.

The more he talked about his New York, the more he wanted to be anchored in this time, at this moment. Never seeing more than a fleeting glimpse of a world was like being able to watch only movie trailers and never the movie. He yearned for roots, to be part of a place, to flow with time's natural pace. Dennis would have bought a one-way ticket back to 2017 if that had been offered, but even stopping in this century would be better than feeling like a seagull blown by a storm without end. He could learn to live in 2300. He could adapt. He looked around the room for something physical to hold on to, to secure him in place, the way a man on a bucking bronco ride looks for the nonexistent horn with ever-increasing desperation as the ride grows more out of control. Holding on tight to something might keep him in place.

Having a connection in 2300, a purpose, might have been the antidote.

Dennis was fatigued from the hopeless task of assembling a jigsaw puzzle from pieces that would never fit together because they came from different puzzles. He wanted to be normal again.

He drank the last of his beer; the alcohol warmed his belly and loosened his tongue. "I wonder if you're real or if I'm hallucinating all of this. A hallucination makes more sense than anything else I've come up with so far."

"You're not hallucinating, Dennis." She held his hand again and rubbed the back of it with her fingers. "Do hallucinations feel like this?"

"How do you know that I'm not hallucinating?" Dennis asked, sidestepping her question.

"Like you said, I'm perceptive. Besides, time travel's impossible, but it may not be impossible forever."

"What do you mean?" Dennis asked. His eyes widened.

"Two years ago there was a huge explosion in a remote part of New Mexico. It was so big that the fireball could be seen for hundreds of kilometers away and the blast was heard nearly 500 kilometers distant. A five-kilometer-square area was destroyed. Now, what could that be?"

"A bomb test?" Dennis suggested.

"Why would anyone test a bomb?" Leah shook her head. "No. The speculation was that it was either a faster-than-light engine or a time travel machine that blew up. That's what *Eyecatch* and *The Economist* wrote." She scooted her chair closer to Dennis and spoke more softly. "Granted, it's pure speculation, but Us was mum about what happened. The force of the explosion meant huge amounts of energy were involved, the kind that exotic phenomena like light speed or time travel would require. Research into time travel doesn't get a lot of attention, but that doesn't mean that Us isn't interested."

"You can travel faster than light now?" Travel to the stars. When Dennis was eight, his dream was to become the first doctor on another planet circling another star. They'd need engineers, farmers, men and women to make babies, and doctors.

"No. Not yet. At least not that anyone knows about. But it looks like that we will be able to soon."

Dennis nodded. Despite his previous thin attempts at self-deception, he couldn't deny that he was traveling through time. But whether it was a natural phenomenon or human intervention that was rushing Dennis into the future, he was now certain that he wasn't hallucinating. All remaining doubt was gone. Leah's hand felt real. Her explanations were lucid. He was in 2300.

And traveling through time was a more palatable alternative to hallucinating.

"I never even asked you what you do. All we've been doing is talking about me."

Leah smiled at Dennis. "Yeah, well you have a lot on your mind, Mr. Time Traveler, so you're forgiven. "I'm an architect."

Dennis' eyes filmed over. He was grateful that napkins were still used in the future. Once he composed himself, he told Leah that his wife had been an architect. She apologized. "It's okay. That was a long time ago," he said, trying to cheer himself up. He took in a quick breath of the alcohol-tasting air, wondering if it was possible to get tipsy just from breathing in here or if that flavored bar air was just a way to encourage customers to buy drinks. "So, in the year 2300, they still need architects?"

"Fortunately, they still do. Computers calculate and draw most of the designs, but humans top off with the finishing touches. It's like making a birthday cake. The cake comes from the factory, but the cake artist makes the cake look pretty. Nobody would buy a plain factory cake. Too ugly and it looks like every other cake. Both human and machine are intertwined. Builder companies like to be able to say that an office, multi-port trans-station, room, school, or something was human-made, even if that's only a flourish." Leah looked at Dennis for a moment before continuing, "Oh. Maybe you don't know what a computer is."

"We have them. People in my time thought that computers were going to take over the world and replace everyone's job."

"They're still trying."

Leah looked at her and Dennis' empty glasses. "Another round?"

"You're still buying?"

Leah nodded.

"How about something to eat, too?" Dennis said as he rubbed his belly.

"Sure. I'll be right back." Dennis watched Leah bounce to the bar. A few minutes later she returned with drinks and a large plate filled with Day-Glo foods. Dennis was about to find out what that food tasted like in 2300.

Leah told Dennis that she hadn't always been a New Yorker, but now she couldn't imagine living anywhere else. She grew up in Boston—had always been a city girl—had attended Harvard, thought about moving to Europe, dismissed the idea, then thought about it again, and did move there. She lived with a guy in Nantes, France for a year before realizing that she had four passions in life: romance, architecture, food, and New York. Probably a dog or cat, too. And travel. Time for reading and relaxing as well. "That's more than four things," Leah said with a chuckle. "And they weren't all compatible."

She and Dennis talked about the differences between New York and Boston—Dennis was surprised to learn that Boston still had many original buildings, that it wasn't filled with skyscrapers like New York. Leah told him about her childhood, her older sister who taught Chinese and Estonian in Chicago, her summers as a camper in Canada that introduced her to the concept of homesickness, her brief flirtation with becoming a professional volleyball player, and a trip with her parents to Paris, where she saw the Eiffel Tower and which made her fall in love with architecture.

"I've always been a brunette with brown eyes," Leah said. "A lot of people change their style, but I've always felt comfortable this way. And you?"

"The options for changing one's looks were a lot more limited in my century. Hair color. Colored contacts. Something called Botox. And endless hours at the gym."

"We like gyms, too," Leah said. "They're free for everyone."

After they finished their third round of drinks and Dennis had polished off every last bit of his colorful food, Leah leaned forward and asked, "I imagine that you have no place to sleep?"

"That's right," Dennis admitted, hoping that Leah at least half-believed his story and didn't take him for a vagrant.

"You're welcome to stay at my place."

"You're sure?"

"I already said that. Come on. Let's go before they turn the heat off."

"Heat off?" Dennis asked, a puzzled look on his face.

"It's January. The outside is heated, but only until 8:00 p.m. Then winter's back. I don't have a coat, and neither do you."

Leah lived five blocks from the bar. During their briskly paced walk, they passed by many oval doors, but Dennis couldn't tell what was behind any of them because none had signage. They made it to Leah's apartment four minutes before the outdoor heat was turned off.

Leah took her shoes off in the front hall, which was a half-step lower than the rest of the apartment, like a Japanese genkan. Dennis took off his shoes, too.

"You can take a shower if you want," Leah said as they walked into her apartment, which was on the 151st floor of a 300-storey mixed residential, office, and recreational building. Folk art sculptures of hybrid animals—half-giraffe, half-dragon, a tiger, and others—were in the nooks of what would have been a bookshelf in his time. They were mythological beasts that reminded Dennis of ancient Greek history. A painting of the Taj Mahal hung in the entry hall, and another painting of the Eiffel Tower took up most of the space on one of the living room walls. On one of the other walls was a photograph of a building that Dennis didn't recognize. It looked like one of the tall, ultramodern skyscrapers in Dubai, only taller, made entirely out of glass and standing tall in the middle of a lush rain forest. All three artworks were framed in wood. Dennis wondered what had happened to the technology of art in electronic frames—perhaps that was just a fad in 2112. Bright spotlights that radiated from the ceiling lit up the art as they walked into the room. Dennis whistled at the opulence. Leah blushed and told Dennis that the rent wasn't expensive in part because this building generated most of its own energy through a combination of solar cells and energy-absorbing wall panels that collected heat from people, pets, hot bath water, and appliances, and in part because her employer subsidized a portion of her rent. "But I do like to be surrounded by pretty things," she said.

"You have good taste."

Leah touched a button on the wall and the Beatles' 'A Hard Day's Night' filled the room. Dennis appreciated what seemed to be the only constant in time.

"Leah."

"Yes?"

"Thank you for saving me."

They locked eyes. Dennis still felt forty, but he could no longer assign a number to it. Leah took Dennis' hand. "You're no longer lost, Dennis. And thank you for making my day special."

"I'd like a shower," Dennis said, feeling the need to shed centuries of grime. "Can I take you up on that offer?"

"The shower's in that room," Leah said, pointing to the far end of the hallway behind Dennis, where another oval door was. "If you can't figure out how it works, shout, and I'll show you. But you're a smart guy, so I think you can. I'm going to do a few yoga stretches and then I'll join you in the shower."

Although confused by Leah's promise to join him, Dennis took off his clothes, stepped into the shower, and surveyed the controls. It wasn't as complicated as a shower he'd once met in a century-old hotel in Barcelona, with its four knobs and pull chain. The controls on Leah's shower were like something he'd expect to see on a starship—futuristic, but still making sense. There were only a limited number of functions to coordinate. Dennis touched the green button, which seemed an obvious first step. A panel lit up, displaying a numerical scale from 10 to 50. Dennis guessed that was either a timer or the temperature in Celsius. He touched 40, and the shower started. Dennis was ready to spring backwards—his cold water defense mechanism—but the water was instantly hot, a pleasing happenstance that he had never encountered before, and which was much better than the many first-coat-the-customer-with-ice showers he'd been in.

Music started as soon as the water did. Dennis didn't recognize the song, but he was struck by the novelty of being able to hear the lyrics, crisply and cleanly, while the water cascaded around him. Every shower radio he'd ever owned sounded like it was broadcasting from under mud.

The water smelled like a garden of lavender, eucalyptus, and raspberries. So natural was the aroma that when Dennis closed his eyes he could see a terraced garden, perfect green grass, long-stemmed roses and sunflowers, and wild berry bushes forming a tunnel through which he walked. He took in longer and longer breaths, letting out an "ah," before the beginning the cycle again.

*When was last the time I slept? I'm so sleepy.* Dennis' eyelids began to succumb to the tug of gravity. His chin touched his chest before snapping back up. His leg muscles, too, felt wobbly, in desperate need of a good night's sleep, or even better, a week's. He knew the symptoms well from his hospital residence days—sixteen-hour shifts during the first year, twenty-four hour shifts during subsequent years— where he had counted the minutes until break time, when he was allowed to squirrel away in a nap room, stretched out on a cot in his hospital uniform, so dead to the world that no dream dared enter his subconscious. He was nearly at his max waking time and would soon be in that nether world where the mind controls the body with diminishing authority until the mind itself is no longer aware. If it weren't for the succulent aroma of meadow and the hot water cascading over his skin, Dennis might have sat down on the shower floor, curled up into a small ball like a sleeping dog, and fallen asleep right there on a bed of grass and flowers. The shower re-energized him—but for how long?

Dennis waited in the shower for Leah. His waterproof watch said ten minutes, then fifteen, then twenty. No Leah. Maybe he'd misheard her when she said that she was going to join him in the shower. Time travel probably caused mental dislocation and he could have mistaken what she actually said—it might have been "I'll see you after the shower." *No, that's wishful thinking.* Leah's words had been unambiguous. Instinctively, Dennis knew what happened, but knowing didn't diminish the hollowness that pitted his bones. He pressed the glossy red button and the shower stopped. Hot, dry air—also smelling of sweet meadow—from all four sides of the shower blew the water off of his body, drying him quickly and completely. He put his clothes back on, the same clothes he had been wearing for 300 years.

*How many years has Leah been dead?*

The bookcases with the art that Leah had collected were gone. The photos and paintings of buildings and places that Leah had enjoyed—vanished. There was furniture and art, but it was alien, it wasn't Leah's, and it held no interest for Dennis. Dennis looked at the new bed and bureau with all the interest of a school kid eying an empty blackboard at the first day of school.

It was time to go. Dennis had no future in this empty apartment. He looked at the wall where Leah's painting of the Eiffel Tower had been, thinking about how that enduring structure had inspired Leah and wishing that he could have learned more about her life and dreams. He walked out of Leah's apartment, more uncertain of his future than ever because for the second time in a day, a locking door closed out a life that he desperately wanted to keep.

There was nobody in the street. Dennis heard his footsteps echo even on the rubbery sidewalk as he rambled through a barren Manhattan. *Maybe the darkness keeps people inside at night in the future.* But that couldn't be: New York was timeless, and no matter what the eon, there should be people hurrying from there to there. New York was and forever would be the city that never sleeps. But tonight the city was mute, even quieter than it had been in carless 2300. Now New York appeared to be a city without cars and people. *Was this it? Am I the only person left in the world? Am I supposed to be Adam? If so, where is my Eve?*

*Or am I a guinea pig in some cosmic experiment gone wrong?*

*When am I?*

Dennis looked around, slowly moving his head up higher and higher, surveying the impossibly steep buildings. Were they the same buildings that had been there before he went into Leah's apartment? If he'd been an architect, Dennis might have noticed, but he couldn't tell what, if anything, had changed in the course of the past hour. Was he still near 2300 or in some far-flung future? A few random apartment windows tried to illuminate the outside. *It's possible there are people in those apartments. It's also possible that this is power recycling at its best and the lights are going to stay lit by themselves for eternity—the punchline of this cosmic joke.* He shivered under the cloudless night sky dotted by stars that offered no heat. But he didn't care. *So be it. If I die on the streets of New York, frozen to death, what will it matter? There's nobody left to mourn and nobody to mourn me.*

Dennis remembered how Leah had opened the door to the bar just by walking into it. He found a similar set of oval doors on the next block. *I might as well try and see what's there. If the doors open, that's where I'll go. If not, I bow to my fate.*

The doors opened, and Dennis followed the warmth inside. The bar was empty and soundless, as if in a ghost town from America's frontier days, now inhabited only by the memories of people who had tried to make something of their lives, but who died destitute and alone. There were no half-heard conversations. No glasses on the tables, no coats hanging on hooks, no bags or objects of any kind that might have belonged to human beings. It smelled stale.

Without warning, a voice from the bar boomed, "How may I help you, friend?" Dennis jumped nearly a foot into the air. *Jesus.* He had to wait for his heart rate to return to normal before he could process thought. *An automated bar? Why not?* Nothing about the future surprised him anymore.

Dennis wanted a drink, but he wanted information even more. "What year is this?"

"It's 2405, friend. How else may I help you? Wouldn't you like a drink?" The woman's voice spoke with perfect clarity and intonation. It didn't sound synthesized at all.

*Three hundred and eighty-eight years.*

Dennis sat down, closed his eyes, and rested his head on his folded arms. His legs melted into the chair, and he no longer had the spirit to fight the tug of gravity against his eyes. He was tired. Tired from traveling. Tired from being an unwilling piece of an enigmatic Rube Goldberg machine whose purpose was clouded by the machine's byzantine parts. Tired from making a friend and losing her just as quickly.

After several minutes, Dennis opened his eyes and sat up. He twisted his body to look around the room to see if anything had changed. Nothing had. "What's your strongest drink?" he asked.

"That would be a Titan Straight," the unseen machine replied.

"How many of those would I have to drink before I was rendered unconscious?"

Silence answered Dennis' question. Maybe the bartender was programmed to call the police when she thought that a customer was going to hurt himself or somebody else. That's what he would have programmed into such a machine because alcohol mixed with an unstable psyche can set in motion a hundred different paths to an accident or death. Dennis reprioritized his options and decided that just a single drink would be enough. "I'll take one Titan Straight," Dennis said, not caring what went into it. There was no acknowledgment from the machine. "A Titan Straight, please," he repeated, glaring in the direction of the voice.

But the machine didn't respond. "Hello? Hello? Are you there?" *Damn. I can't even get a drink now.*

The door opened. Sunlight burned Dennis' eyes. Strong oranges and yellows angled along the horizon, reflecting off of the myriad glass and metal towers that grew out of Manhattan's fertile ground. It was daytime again. Dennis felt the relatively cool inside air blend with a hot outdoor atmosphere. *It's not January anymore.*

"Hello, Dr. Tanner," the woman said. Dennis looked at the two middle-aged visitors, a man and a woman. Both had dark hair, straddling that indeterminate color zone between brown and black, like an exotic Turkish tea. Their features were a combination of Hispanic and Asian, along with something he couldn't identify—Middle Eastern? African? Dennis noticed that they each had one green and one blue eye. They were both thin and tall, appearing a little over six feet to Dennis' squinting eyes. "Welcome," she said.

"Welcome to where?" Dennis asked.

"To 2418," the woman replied. "I'm Holly. This is Gian. We're glad you made it. We need you."

"I don't understand."

Holly gave Dennis a silver bottle. "Here, something to drink in case you're thirsty. Would you like water? Tea? Fruit water?"

His mouth did feel parched. "Just water would be fine." She ran her hand horizontally across the bottle, which changed from silver to clear. The liquid inside changed from dark green to clear. Holly handed the bottle to Dennis.

Dennis emptied it quickly and completely. When he was finished, he said, "You need me? I don't understand anything about why I'm here or how I got here. Except that I gather that the two of you brought me to 2418."

"Yes, we and our team. We brought you here because you're a doctor, a surgeon. We have few medical specialists, so we transported you from the past to the present," Holly said. "You've had a difficult, disjointed, and undoubtedly confusing journey, but we had to move you forward in intervals. Stop-and-go time travel. Energy barriers along the way prevent us from time traveling you here all at once."

Answers, finally. Dennis sighed. Answers were like morphine, blocking the pain of uncertainty that had been ravaging his mind.

*What gave you the right to steal my life, to take away everything that I loved and knew? What gave you people the hubris and audacity to destroy my life to save your own? You had no right to transport me to the future without my permission, and would I have given that? No. The people in the future aren't any more important than I am, than my life with Rachel had been.* But Dennis was too tired to vocalize his rage. Anger took energy and Dennis had precious little of that left. Maybe anger would come tomorrow. For now, the fire in his belly was extinguished by the power of sheer exhaustion.

"Why me?" he asked finally. "There are better surgeons, I'm sure. Somebody who was born closer to your time would have been a smarter choice. They would know more advanced medicine, for one thing." Endless questions sped through his brain all at once, like cars on a highway jockeying for the fast lane, but he asked this big one next: "What happened to your doctors?"

"Most of our doctors are dead," Holly said. She paused for a few seconds to let those words sink in before continuing, "Not only the doctors but almost all professionals died. Years ago, we started deploying genetic tools to increase our brain power. Not everyone's brain power, just those who were in fields in which thought was their primary tool, such as doctors, world leaders, physicists, chemists, architects, engineers, experimenters, biologists. It worked, too. We became smarter.

"But the enhancements also killed. Not at first, but over time the manipulated genes altered the genomes in unanticipated ways. The consequences of our misreading DNA were deadly—almost everyone whose brain was enhanced died. The malformed genes also worked their way into sperm and eggs. The smartest people most likely to make the smartest children could no longer could have any. Society can't function for long without its thinkers and leaders. Without doctors to cure and biologists to make medicines. Without politicians to guide us. Without engineers to build and chemists to create new materials. We are a world spinning toward self-annihilation."

She studied Dennis to see if he was absorbing all of this. "The same therapy also killed many of the scientists who were working on figuring out time travel. We almost doomed ourselves. We were terrified."

Holly and Gian finally sat down. Holly pulled out another bottle from her bag, swiped her finger across the outside and then drank the orange liquid.

"You're a good surgeon. Not the best, of course, but you also happen to have been in the right place at the right time. Because we had to transport you to the present in multiple jumps, we chose people like you, who started out in stable locations and whom we hoped would continue to move forward from stable location to stable location. If you had lived in an old, wooden house that would have succumbed to the elements in twenty years, we wouldn't have picked you. Because you lived in a building that we knew would stand for at least another hundred years, we could start you on the way to 2418, knowing that you would survive at least partway to our time. The rest would be up to chance."

"I see. I think." There was so much to absorb. Dennis waited a couple of seconds before asking, "There are others from the past?"

"Yes," Holly said. "So far sixty-one have arrived successfully. It takes enormous amounts of energy and months of planning to bring somebody here from the past. Less than a quarter make it because every stop along the way is a danger. At the end of every jump interval, there's a chance that the traveler and random matter will occupy the same space. Most people we time traveled ended up inside of walls or under trucks, drowned, or had some other unfortunate accident. We've lost good physicians, engineers, leaders. We are blue about those people."

"Oh," was all Dennis could say. But then he thought of something else. "Where is everyone? New York is so empty."

"There's more to tell you, but not now. Tonight you'll rest, and tomorrow you'll start work. We have hospitals with many patients but few surgeons. Do you feel like getting right to work?"

Anger still boiled inside Dennis, like a pot of water left too long on the stove. *They took my love away from me.* Dennis wanted to unleash his fury against these people. He wanted to call them what they were, kidnappers and jailers. He wanted to shout the vilest words he knew at them, slam his fists on the table, hit them. Hurt them. His anger grew, but then it abated once again. He wasn't sure why he went from outrage to calm in less time that it took to make one of those time leaps. But calm felt better than wrath. His entire adult life he had been saving people, sacrificing his sleep, his time, even his freedom to be the best surgeon he could. Now he would be helping people in ways that he could never have imagined. Maybe 2418 was a gift.

Dennis wanted to get back to fixing people. He needed that as much as patients needed him. And he wanted to stop traveling more than anything else.

Yes, his hundred other questions could wait. All Dennis wanted to do now was lie down and close his eyes; no traveler had ever been wearier. He'd be in sleep's arms soon. Tomorrow he'd learn about this new world and begin contributing to it. And for as long as he lived, he'd never forget the people he had shared his life with.

The doors opened again, and another strong burst of sunlight blurred Dennis' vision for an instant. Another tall, mixed-ethnicity man, also with tea-colored hair and two different-colored eyes walked in, silhouetted against the bright sunshine, as though a halo surrounded him. Standing to his right was a shorter woman.

"Leah!"

"Hey," Leah said, waving to Dennis, her hand forming a perfect 180-degree arc.

"Are you—did you come from—?"

"Yep. From 2300. They need me, too. Fancy that."

"Who are you?" the President demanded of the woman who had materialized in his bedroom. He threw back the blanket and bolted upright; his frock of white hair moved in the opposite direction. He pointed at the intruder. "Wait. I recognize you. You're Mary Wells, the forty-seventh president, thirty-two years ago." He withdrew his finger. "Or somebody who looks like her. How did you get in here?" The President leaned to the right and pressed the emergency button by the side of his bed.

President Wells anxiously surveyed her bedroom. Abraham Lincoln's painting had been replaced by one of Benjamin Franklin. *Who would have changed the art without asking me?* The room's color was a deeper blue than it had been just moments ago, and the room smelled of pine. The horse-patterned blanket that was crumpled around the man's legs wasn't her blanket. There were other things, too: the curtains, the clock on the night table, the telephone, the floor rug—they were all wrong. Wells started to ask the intruder in her bed—the President of the United States' bed—*who the hell are you*, but before she could say anything, the man vanished, and her bedroom changed again.

# No Time to Say Goodbye
## by Marina V.

Singer songwriter Marina V composed and sings the theme song to No Time to Say Goodbye. Your can hear the song on YouTube at http://bit.ly/NTSGsong, and, of course on Marina V's website, www.MarinaV.com.

> Only yesterday
> It all made sense to me
> It all made sense to me
> Should we accept our fate,
> Bow to the enemy?
> Is time my enemy?
>
> Capricious winds
> Blow us through time
> And life's regrets surround my mind
> A fading glimpse
> That's all I have left of us
>
> There's no time to lose
> There's no time to cry
> There are no answers to how or why
> We are here somehow
> There's only here and now
> There's no time to cry
> No time to say goodbye

# NO TIME TO SAY GOODBYE

It was a life ago
It seems like yesterday
Was it just yesterday


Capricious winds
Blow us through time
And life's regrets surround my mind
A fading glimpse
That's all I have left of us


There's no time to lose
There's no time to cry
There are no answers to how or why
We are here somehow
There's only here and now
There's no time to cry
No time to say goodbye


And when my future is my past

I will know

# Acknowledgements

Thanks to Chris, Mara, and Debbie O'Byrne of JETLAUNCH (www.jetlaunch.net) for their invaluable help in bringing this book from manuscript to your hands.

*No Time to Say Goodbye* would not have been possible without the thoughtful attention of Claren Books' editor, Sarah Doebereiner.

The following all offered invaluable insights and suggestions:
Larry Kahaner (www.kahaner.com)
Steph VanderMeulen (www.stephvandermeulen.com)
Morgen Bailey (morgenbailey.wordpress.com)

I couldn't have done this without them.

# Afterword

Did you enjoy *No Time to Say Goodbye*? Could you take a few minutes and review *No Time to Say Goodbye* on Amazon, Goodreads, or your blog? (Or even a tweet would be terrific.) Your review will help spread the word about my book. Independent authors rely on reader reviews like yours. Thanks, and I'm glad I could share *No Time to Say Goodbye* with you.

You can find out more about Bill Adler Jr. on his website, www.adlerbooks.com. He tweets at @billadler.

www.ingramcontent.com/pod-product-compliance
Lightning Source LLC
Chambersburg PA
CBHW071208130626
46555CB00004B/1627